W9-BPS-026

Regina Public Library
BOOK SALE ITEM
Non-returnable

DINO-MIKE
AND THE
DINOSAUR
DOOMSDAY

WRITTEN & ILLUSTRATED BY FRANCO

STONE ARCH BOOKS
a capstone imprint

Regina Public Library
BOOK SALE ITEM
Non-returnable

Dino-Mike! is published by
Stone Arch Books,
a Capstone imprint
1710 Roe Crest Drive
North Mankato, Minnesota 56003
www.mycapstone.com

Copyright © 2016 by Stone Arch Books

All rights reserved. No part of this publication may
be reproduced in whole or in part, or stored in a
retrieval system, or transmitted in any form or
by any means, electronic, mechanical, photocopying,
recording, or otherwise, without written permission
of the publisher.

Cataloging-in-Publication Data is available on
the Library of Congress website.

ISBN: 978-1-4965-2491-1 (library hardcover)
ISBN: 978-1-4965-2495-9 (paperback)
ISBN: 978-1-4965-2499-7 (eBook)

Summary: To find the evil Mr. Bones, Dino-Mike
and Shannon will have to follow the fossils — even if
it leads them to an ancient dinosaur graveyard
in Antarctica!

Printed in China.
1468

CONTENTS

Young Mike Evans travels the world with his dino-hunting dad and his best friend, Shannon. From the Jurassic Coast in Great Britain to the Liaoning Province in China, young Dino-Mike has been there, *dug* that!

When his dad is dusting fossils, Mike's boning up on his own dino skills — only he's finding the real deal. A live T. rex egg! A portal to the Jurassic Period!! An undersea dinosaur sanctuary!!!

Prepare yourself for another wild and wacky Dino-Mike adventure, which nobody will ever believe . . .

Chapter 1
COLD CASE

"Why are we here again?" Mike Evans asked through chattering teeth. He stared out at the bright white sheet of ice, stretching to the horizon. "This place is a winter wasteland."

"Actually, Mike," interrupted his newfound friend and dino-adventuring sidekick, Shannon, "right now, it's summer in Antarctica."

Mike rolled his eyes and sighed. "That's the tenth time you've told me that!"

"Then I probably already told you that Antarctica isn't a wasteland at all," she added. "It's actually considered a desert."

"Yep, you told me that too," said Mike, annoyed. "But there's no way this place is a desert, Shannon. My teeth wouldn't be chattering this much if I was in the Mojave!"

"Oh, stop being such a wimp, Dino-Mike!" came a familiar voice.

Mike spun around and spotted his archenemy standing in the doorway of the scientific base camp.

"Jurassic Jeff," he grumbled.

Actually, Jeff was no longer Mike's worst enemy — but he wasn't his favorite person either. Shannon's older brother was super smart (he once brought dinosaurs back to the present day, after all), but his intelligence could be incredibly helpful or incredibly harmful. Dino-Mike just hoped Jeff hadn't woken up on the wrong side of the bunk this morning.

"Who are you calling a wimp, Jeff?" asked Mike. "Didn't you refuse to come on our last expedition to Australia because of all the spiders and snakes?"

Jurassic Jeff folded his arms across his chest and let out a "humph."

"And speaking of Australia," added Mike, turning to Shannon, "that's a continent with proper deserts, not ones covered in snow and ice."

BARK! BARK! BARK! Suddenly, a striped, four-legged beast came bounding across the ice toward the trio.

"Is that a, uh . . . TIGER?!" yelled Jurassic Jeff in a panic.

"HAHA!" Mike and Shannon laughed.

As the beast approached, Mike bent down and patted it on the head. "It's only Ahfu," Mike told Jeff as the dog wagged his tongue and tail happily.

"What did you do to him?" Jeff asked.

"Dad made him a custom heat suit, so he wouldn't freeze out here," Shannon explained. "It's made out of the same high-tech material as our own snowsuits."

When they arrived in Antarctica, Mike, Shannon, and Jeff each received a specially designed heat suit. The suits were made from an ultrathin material created by Shannon and Jeff's father, Dr. Broome.

Dr. Broome had also created Mike's beloved, gadget-filled Dino Jacket. The jacket had saved Mike's life many times during his dino-tracking adventures.

"I suggested we add the tiger stripes. Isn't he scary?" asked Mike, smirking.

Jurassic Jeff kneeled down and lovingly squeezed Ahfu's shmushy face. "Yes, you are . . . yes, you are . . . You are such a scary-wary doggie." Ahfu excitedly licked Jeff's lips, over and over. Jeff laughed with delight.

"Ew!" squealed Mike and Shannon, wrinkling their noses.

"What?" asked Jeff, looking up from the slobbery kisses.

"Okay, maybe Ahfu isn't so scary," Mike admitted, "but his former owners are still on the prowl."

Dino-Mike and the gang had first met Ahfu on their dino-tracking expedition in China. It was there that they also discovered that Ahfu's former owner, Ms. Li Jing, was part of an evil duo known as Mr. and Ms. Bones!

"Do you think Mr. and Ms. Bones will be coming to Antarctica?" Jeff asked Dino-Mike.

"If they're looking for whole, intact dinosaur skeletons, this would be the perfect place to find them," Mike replied.

Since there wasn't much to do in Antarctica, Mike's dad, a world-famous paleontologist, had given his son plenty of reading material. Dino-Mike had been studying up on the continent.

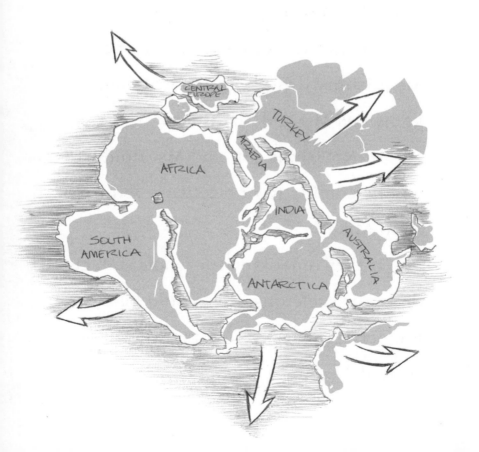

He learned that millions of years ago, Australia, South America, and Antarctica were all one big piece of land called Gondwana. If dinosaur fossils existed in Australia, they'd be here too. But digging them out of the mile-thick ice was nearly impossible — except for Mr. and Ms. Bones! With their technology, they'd be able to bring any fossils back to life.

Even a high-tech heat suit couldn't stop the chill going down Mike's spine at that thought.

"Hello, Jeffrey," came a voice. "Good to see you again."

Jeff turned and spotted a man walking up the hill from the airport runway.

"Hey, Dr. Evans," said Jeff, greeting Mike's dad. "Glad you could make it."

Dr. Evans set down his suitcases and shook Jeff's hand. Coming up behind him was a shorter man.

"I'd like you to meet Dr. S. R. Jiang," said Dr. Evans.

"Nice to meet you, sir," said Jeff, shaking the doctor's hand. "I hope the plane ride was pleasant."

"Pleasant enough," replied Dr. Jiang.

"I apologize for my father not being here," said Jeff. "He rarely leaves the house anymore."

"No need to apologize," said Dr. Jiang. "I worked with your father many years ago, before you and your sister were born. A strange man, but very nice and very brilliant."

"I'll tell him you said so," said Jeff. "Now let me show you where you'll be staying." Jeff picked up Dr. Jiang's bags and led him toward the base camp.

Dr. Evans lagged behind to speak with Mike. "I don't want you two wandering off again and getting into trouble," his dad told him. "Dr. Jiang and I have lots of work to do and only a few days to do it. You probably won't be seeing much of us."

"Don't worry, Dad," Mike assured him. "How could we get into trouble?" Dino-Mike pointed out at the endless snow and ice. "There's nothing around for miles."

"That's exactly what I wanted to hear," Dr. Evans said, patting the top of Dino-Mike's hood.

Dr. Evans picked up his luggage and headed toward the base camp. "The plane will be back in a few days to pick us up," he said.

Mike and Shannon were left alone with Ahfu. They watched as the plane that had brought them took off from a nearby runway.

"Well," Shannon began, "like it or not, we're stuck here for a few days."

"What could possibly go wrong?" Mike said with a smirk.

Chapter 2

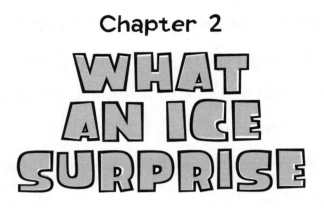

WHAT AN ICE SURPRISE

"The penguins definitely know it's summer here!" Dino-Mike exclaimed.

He and Shannon had hiked up an icy ridge. Far below, they watched thousands of emperor penguins dive in and out of the water, splishing and splashing like kids at a swimming pool.

"Hey, guys," said Jeff, hiking up to join them. "What are you doing?"

"Just checking out the penguins," Shannon answered.

"Did they give you any ideas for what we should do about the Bones twins?" asked Jeff, plopping down beside them on the icy ridge.

"They're not twins, Jeff," said Shannon. "They're just brother and sister."

"Whatever. Same difference," said Jeff. "Whether they're twins or not doesn't matter. We can still use their relationship to our advantage."

"How?" ask Dino-Mike, puzzled, although Shannon already seemed to know the answer.

"Brothers and sisters fight," Jeff explained. "If we can pit them against each other, we might be able to gain the advantage."

"How are you so sure that they'll fight?" asked Mike.

"Trust us," Shannon and Jeff said together.

"I'm afraid they may be right," came a voice from behind them.

Climbing up the ridge was Dr. Jiang. Mike looked to see if his father was with him. Dr. Jiang noticed and said, "Do not fear, your father is still in the lab."

"Then what are you doing here?" asked Dino-Mike.

"The siblings you seek argued almost constantly when they were children," Dr. Jiang explained. "They have strong opinions. Unfortunately, most of their opinions are wrong."

"How do you know that?" asked Shannon, confused.

"I'm afraid I must confess something." Dr. Jiang took a deep breath and then said, "The Bones siblings are my children."

"Whaaaaat?!" Mike, Shannon, and Jeff exclaimed together.

"They carry a deep-seated anger toward your father," added Dr. Jiang.

"But why?" Shannon asked.

Dr. Jiang dug his hands into the pockets of his winter jacket. He looked somewhat sad.

"As I stated before, Dr. Broome and I worked together many years ago," he explained. "During this time, your father discovered the gem that powers the Jurassic Portal. It was his discovery — his alone. Not mine. But my children feel they have some right to the discovery and some right to profit from it."

"My dad isn't a scientist for the money!" Shannon exclaimed. "He wants his research to help people — and animals — all over the world."

"That's exactly why I'm glad he found the portal gem first," said Dr. Jiang. "I'm glad your father has control over it. He is a good and honest man."

"Then how do we stop your children from taking it from him?" Dino-Mike interrupted.

"I don't know," answered Dr. Jiang. "I haven't spoken with my children in years, and I doubt they'd listen anyway."

RUMMBBBBLLE!

"What was that?!" Jurassic Jeff exclaimed.

RUMMBBBBLLE!

The ground beneath Dino-Mike's feet suddenly shook — again and again.

RUMMBBBBLLE!

The group quickly scurried toward the edge of the ridge. Below, nearly all of the emperor penguins were gone!

The penguins had hidden deep in the water. Something had frightened them off the ice.

As the group looked on, the ice sheet near the base camp began to crack.

KA-BOOOM!

Rocks and ice chunks exploded into the sky. As the ground shook more violently, snow and ice on the hill near the camp gave way.

FWOOSH!

An avalanche poured down on the base, covering it completely.

"Oh no!" Mike exclaimed.

His father was trapped!

Chapter 3

BONES REVEALED

RUMMBBBBLLE!

The ground near the base camp
continued to shake, bubble, and steam.
Then, out of the destruction, stepped
two figures dressed in black.

"Get down!" yelled Jeff, pulling his
sister, Shannon, to the ground. Mike and
Dr. Jiang followed their lead.

"But my dad!" Mike exclaimed, his
face half-buried in the snow.

"Shhh," whispered Jeff. "He's
okay. That bunker could withstand an
earthquake. It's probably the safest place
on this entire sheet of ice."

Jeff peered over the ridge to look at
the figures below.

"It's them all right," Jeff confirmed. "The Bones twins are back."

"They're not twins!" everyone else said back at him.

"Twins, siblings, whatever!" Jeff replied. "All I know is that they buried the base camp on purpose. They probably think we're all trapped in there, so we have at least one advantage."

"Yeah, what's that?" asked Dino-Mike.

"The element of surprise," said Jeff.

"And how do we use that to our advantage?" Mike pressed.

"We wait until the Bones leave and think no one is following them and then . . . we follow them," Jeff replied.

Jurassic Jeff might have been super smart, but this definitely wasn't his smartest of plans.

BZZZZZT!

Just then, Dino-Mike's high-tech hoodie started buzzing. Mike knew that his jacket was equipped with a two-way communication device, but only one person knew the number. And that person was —

"DAD?!" Mike shouted, pressing the Speak button on the cuff of his coat. "Hello? Dad?" he repeated.

Dino-Mike looked down at the base camp and spotted something he hadn't seen before.

Sticking out from beneath the avalanche of snow was the camp's satellite antennae!

After a moment, the crackling voice of Mike's dad came through, loud and clear. "No, Dad, we're all fine out here," Dino-Mike answered. "Yes, we were far enough from the snow slide that we didn't get caught in it." He listened again. "Okay, Dad. Okay. We will, Dad."

Mike pressed the Disconnect button on his jacket and turned to the group. "My dad says there's no way in or out of base camp right now," Mike explained. "He says we should head to the emergency bunker for the night."

"Good thinking," said Jeff, but then he headed in the opposite direction of the bunker. "Too bad we already have other plans."

Chapter 4

DOOMSDAY DINOSAUR

"Why is there so much snow here?" Mike blurted out as the group traveled along an icy ridge.

"Well, actually —" began Shannon.

Dino-Mike and Jurassic Jeff both rolled their eyes and sighed.

"I know you don't really want an answer," Shannon continued, "but it's not the snow so much as the ice. Did you know that ninety percent of the ice formed on Earth is found in Antarctica?"

"That's it!" Dino-Mike exclaimed.

"Shannon, you're a genius!"

"I am?" she asked, puzzled.

"She is?" Jurassic Jeff added.

Dr. Jiang stood nearby, rubbing his chin. "I might know what you're thinking, but please, do tell the others."

"Dinosaurs lived in warm, tropical climates," Mike explained.

"Yeah, so?" questioned Shannon and Jeff.

"They wouldn't last a minute in these temps," said Dino-Mike.

"If the Bones siblings somehow managed to bring a dinosaur to life," Mike added, "it'd be frozen solid faster than you can say velociraptor."

"Well, that's not entirely correct," Shannon pointed out. "You've obviously forgotten about the polar dinosaurs."

"Or burrowing dinosaurs," added Dr. Jiang.

Mike scrunched his face. He was afraid to admit that he still had a lot to learn about dinosaurs.

"Still, you could be on to something, Mike," suggested Dr. Jiang. "A large majority of dinosaurs never would have survived in these conditions.

"If my children plan to bring a dinosaur back to life," the doctor added, "let's hope they knitted it an XL-sized sweater."

"Don't you mean xenoceratops-sized?" Jurassic Jeff joked.

Mike and Shannon laughed.

"Look!" Dr. Jiang suddenly interrupted. He pointed toward the setting sun on the horizon. In its shadow stood two silhouetted figures — the Bones siblings!

"Why are they dancing?" asked Jeff.

The siblings, still wearing all black, danced in circles until the sun completely set, and the sky grew dark.

Then, they each pulled several small, golf-ball-sized orbs from their pockets. The orbs glowed with neon light.

"What are those?" Dino-Mike asked Dr. Jiang.

Before the doctor could answer, the orbs sprouted mechanical wings and then lifted into the sky.

They zigged and zagged through the air, glowing like —

"Fireflies," Dr. Jiang muttered through his teeth.

"Huh?" Shannon asked, confused.

HOWWWWWWWWWL!!

Ahfu startled the group with a sudden howl.

They had nearly forgotten about the
dog, although he'd been trailing right
behind them for the past three hours.

BARK! BARK! BARK! Ahfu warned.

"What is it, boy?" asked Jurassic Jeff,
kneeling. As he did, he felt the ground
begin to rumble again. "An earthquake?"
Jeff wondered aloud.

"No," said Shannon, "a dinosaur!"

Mike and Shannon had witnessed
the Boneses unearth a real-life dinosaur
before, but this seemed different.
The shaking and rumbling was
more powerful than anything they'd
experienced in China.

CRAAAAAACK!

A giant zigzagging crack in the ice sheet began at the horizon and raced toward them like lightning.

"Look out!" shouted Jurassic Jeff.

The group scrambled for safety, but it was too late. The ground beneath their feet opened up. **CRUNNNNNCH!** A geyser of ice thrust them thirty feet into the air.

Shannon slipped and started to fall from the rising ice sheet.

"Help!" she screamed.

Without hesitating, Dino-Mike pressed a button inside the lining of his high-tech Dino Jacket. **FWIP!**

A grapnel hook shot out of his sleeve like a cannon.

It zipped through the air attached to a wire. Then, **SNAP!** The grapnel hook snagged Shannon out of the sky like a raptor claw.

Pressing another button, Dino-Mike quickly reeled her back to safety.

Well, actually, they were anywhere but safe. Glancing around, Mike quickly realized that they weren't standing on the ice sheet anymore.

They were standing atop a colossal DINOSAUR — the biggest one Mike had ever seen (in real life or at a museum)!

"Argentinosaurus," Dr. Jiang muttered.

"Argentinosaurus?" repeated Jurassic Jeff. "Isn't that the —"

"Yep," interrupted Shannon, "the Doomsday Dinosaur!"

"Why do they call it that?" asked Mike.

Shannon steadied herself as the dinosaur began to grunt and shake. "I think you're about to find out!"

GAAAAAAARRRRRRRR!!!

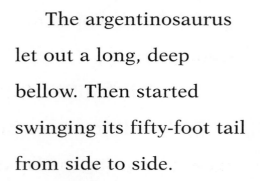

The argentinosaurus let out a long, deep bellow. Then started swinging its fifty-foot tail from side to side.

FWOOSH! FWOOSH!

49

Judging by the argentinosaurus's size, Mike didn't believe this dinosaur was a carnivore. However, even if the dino wouldn't eat them, it could still do some major damage. One swipe from its powerful tail would send them flying a mile through the air.

Dino-Mike needed a plan — and fast!

BARK! BARK! BARK! Ahfu ran excitedly beneath Dino-Mike's feet. The scruffy pup slid and slipped on the dinosaur's smooth scales.

"That's it!" Mike cried out.

Dino-Mike removed his beloved Dino Jacket, throwing the hoodie down on the back of the dinosaur.

Then he pressed a button on the hoodie's lining. **FWWOOP!** The Dino Jacket quickly filled with air, inflating like a portable life raft.

"Get on!" Dino-Mike shouted.

Shannon and Jurassic Jeff looked a bit unsure, but they didn't put up a fight. They hopped into the makeshift sled, followed by Dr. Jiang, Mike, and finally Ahfu.

"Now push!" Mike instructed.

Like a bobsledding team, everyone pushed with their hands to get the jacket moving beneath them. Soon, they were sliding down the back of the dino, faster than a sled on a snowy mountain.

Faster and faster they slid until they neared the end of the dinosaur's tail, which hovered thirty feet off the ground.

"Um, Mike?" asked Shannon. "Any idea how we stop this thing?"

"We don't," Mike replied.

"HUH?!" the others cried out.

"Just hang on!" Mike instructed.

FWOOOOOOOSH!

The makeshift sled rocketed off the end of the dino's tail, flying through the air like a stunt rider off a ramp.

Then, **FWUMP!** The sled crashed down on the icy ground. The puffy Dino Jacket cushioned the landing like an airbag.

"Is everyone okay?" Mike asked.

Jurassic Jeff, Shannon, and Dr. Jiang each gave a nod.

BARK! BARK! BARK!

Ahfu barked excitedly.

"What is it, boy?" Mike said, patting the dog's head. Then he looked up.

"That's my dog!" said an evil masked figure standing over them.

Chapter 5

ARGENTINOSAURUS ATTACK!

The Bones siblings!

Li Jing Jiang and Chiang Jiang stood on either side of the group. They wore black suits, gloves, and skeleton masks.

"That's my dog, and I want him back!" Li Jing shouted.

Shannon stood between Ahfu and Li Jing. "You gave up the right to such a kind animal the minute you showed everyone what a meanie you really are!" Shannon shouted back.

"Uh, guys?" Jeff began.

"No, Jeff!" Shannon stopped him. "Let me finish!"

"I don't need a lecture on how to treat animals," Li Jing told Shannon.

"Oh, really?" said Shannon angrily. "Bringing back dinosaurs and having them cause havoc and threaten people is your idea of being a responsible pet owner?"

"Um, Shannon," Jeff tried to interrupt again.

"Not now!!" shouted Shannon and Li Jing together.

"I'm sorry," said Jeff, "but I just need to say that we should probably —"

"RUN!!" shouted Shannon, finally noticing what Jeff had been trying to warn them about.

The argentinosaurus had raised its massive tail into the air directly above them. Dino-Mike wasn't a physics expert, but he knew that what goes up, must come down. And did it ever! He barely had time to deflate his Dino Jacket and quickly put it on.

As the group all scattered in different directions, the tail came crashing down like a massive redwood tree.

CRAAAAASSSSSH! Dino-Mike and the others lost their footing as the icy earth shook beneath them.

"Dr. Jiang, are you all right?" asked Jeff, picking him up off the ground.

"Yes, I am fine," said Dr. Jiang, "for the moment." The doctor pointed toward the sky. The argentinosaurus lifted his tail high above them again.

Dino-Mike looked up at the dinosaur and tried to think of some way out of the situation. He noticed the mechanical fireflies swirling around the beast. Mike also noticed that the glowing orbs moved whenever the dinosaur did.

He knew what he had to do.

"You guys, run!" commanded Mike. "I'll keep them busy." He started running straight toward the giant beast.

"No!" Shannon shouted in protest.

"We don't have time to argue, Shannon!" Mike yelled back at her.

Mike sprinted at the argentinosaurus. The dino prepared to bring his tail down on top of him. In a panic, Mike put up his hands and yelled, "STOP!"

To his amazement, the dinosaur suddenly froze!

Did that actually work? Dino-Mike wondered.

Then Dino-Mike noticed the Bones siblings standing nearby. They also had their hands raised into the air, and their black, high-tech gloves glowed with electric energy.

Together with the gloves, Mike knew that they could control the dinosaur however they wanted. But then, why did they choose to stop it?

"Dad?" Mike heard the Bones twins say together. Dino-Mike followed their gaze to Dr. Jiang.

"What are you doing here?" asked Li Jing. She pulled off her skull mask but continued holding her other hand in the air.

"I could ask you the same question," replied Dr. Jiang. "Why are my son and daughter bringing old fossils to life around the world? Why are they terrorizing people with dinosaurs?"

"You know why, old man!" shouted his son, Chiang Jiang. "Dr. Broome stole everything from you, and you never did anything about it!"

"That is not the truth, my son," said Dr. Jiang.

"It is!" Chiang Jiang exclaimed. "He took all the credit! Everything Dr. Broome and his family have become famous for, you should be famous for!"

"My children, Dr. Broome is a good man," their father tried to explain. "He has helped many people with all of his technology and money."

"You see!" Chiang Jiang shouted at his sister. "It's useless talking to him. This is why we put our own plan into action and why we have to do this!"

Chiang Jiang forcefully thrust his gloved palm at his father.

The argentinosaurus lurched forward but then stopped. Chiang Jiang looked over at his sister. Her hand was still raised above her head.

"Do it!" he told her. "NOW!"

Li Jing followed her brother's lead and thrust her hand toward her father. This time, the argentinosaurus ran full steam at Dr. Jiang.

Hmm, thought Mike. *The Boneses only have control over the dinosaur if they both work together.*

Dino-Mike needed to get at least one of those suits away from the siblings.

"Everybody run . . . AGAIN!!" shouted Jurassic Jeff.

"Everyone split up!" added Dino-Mike. "The dinosaur can't chase all of us if we fan out in different directions."

Just then, Mike spotted the tiny floating spheres following along with the dinosaur. *The heat source!* Mike suddenly remembered his idea.

"Keep an eye on the Bones twins," he called over to Shannon. "I'm going to try something."

As the others ran away from the argentinosaurus, Mike ran toward it.

WHAM! The dinosaur's tail came down with a thundering blow, narrowly missing Dino-Mike . . . just as he had hoped!

With a running leap, Mike jumped onto the beast's thick tail. Then he ran up the tail, where moments ago he was sliding down. As he ran, Mike pressed a button on his Dino Jacket's zipper.

FWIP! FWIP! FWIP! Several stegosaurus-like plates burst out of the back of the high-tech hoodie.

Blue lights exploded from the plates in an electric arc.

ZRRRRRRT!

The stegosaurus-like plates were designed to absorb energy, like sunlight through a solar panel, and generate heat for the jacket. Through trial (and a whole lot of error), Mike had learned that the plates could absorb energy from anything giving off heat, like —

"Fireflies," Dino-Mike muttered to himself.

Mike realized that the Bones siblings had been using the mechanical, glowing orbs to keep the dinosaur warm and alive. He didn't want to harm the argentinosaurus. But if he could drain the energy from the fireflies, maybe the cold would shock the dinosaur out of the Boneses' control.

Dino-Mike activated the plates. They glowed with a bluish light. He could feel the plates tracking the heat spheres overhead. Then, blue electric-like arcs of energy shot out from the plates in all directions.

ZZZZZZRRRRRT!

The blue arcs latched onto the buzzing, heat-generating fireflies and sucked the energy out of them. The orbs quickly dimmed and fell from the sky.

The argentinosaurus stopped.

Mike looked down and could see the Bones siblings frantically moving their hands to get the dinosaur moving again.

His idea had worked! The cold snapped the dino out of the Boneses' control. But moments later, the dinosaur beneath Mike began to shiver and shake. The beast bucked like a wild bronco.

Dino-Mike could barely hold on!

Out of the corner of his eye, Mike saw Chiang Jiang pull a familiar device from his pocket. It looked like a TV remote control, but Mike knew the device was much more than that. The Boneses had used a similar gadget in China and Australia to blast dinosaurs — and everything around them — back to the past.

Unless he wanted to end up in the Jurassic Age, Dino-Mike needed to move.

He quickly steadied himself, bent his knees, and then leaped from the dinosaur's back toward the icy ground below. **FWOOSH!**

Chapter 6

BURROWING DINOSAURS

BEEP! BEEP! BEEP! Chiang Jiang
flicked a switch on the controller, and a
warning sounded.

A split second later, **FWOOOOOOSH!** A
hurricane-force wind ripped across the
landscape. A sideways tornado of air
opened into an interdimensional portal,
sucking the argentinosaurus inside.

POP!

Like that, the dinosaur was gone.

At the same time, Dino-Mike landed
on the ice — HARD! "Ugh," he groaned,
rolling and squirming in pain.

Shannon, Jurassic Jeff, and Dr. Jiang rushed to his side. Ahfu barked along behind them.

"You did it!" cried Jeff. "You got them to send the dinosaur back to the past!"

"We don't know where it went," Dino-Mike reminded Jurassic Jeff.

"Well, at least we're all safe," Shannon said.

BARK! BARK! BARK! Just then, Ahfu barked another warning.

Mike turned his attention back to the Bones siblings. They were releasing more mechanical fireflies, which burrowed into the ground this time.

More heat sources for another dinosaur, thought Mike. "I think you may have spoken too soon," he told Shannon.

Then the siblings started dancing, and the ground shook again. **RUMMMBLE!!** Mike and his group prepared for a huge section of the ground to open up and another colossal dinosaur to rise from the earth. A big section didn't open this time, but a bunch of little sections did! Eight to be exact. And out of the earth came eight car-sized dinosaurs!

Before Dino-Mike could even come up with a plan, the dinosaurs disappeared beneath the ice again.

"What the —?" Mike exclaimed, confused. "Where did they go?"

"Oryctodromeus cubicularis," muttered Jurassic Jeff.

"Huh?" Mike asked.

"Burrowing dinosaurs," Shannon explained.

Mike looked at the ground where the dinosaurs had been and spotted the evidence: eight holes in the frozen earth. They had all dug into the ice at the command of the Bones siblings.

Dino-Mike surveyed the ground around him. He was anticipating that any one of the eight dinosaurs could pop up out of the ice at any time.

"Mike! Stay close!" Shannon shouted. "We have no idea where they'll come up next!"

Mike reached back for Shannon's hand as he kept his eyes on the ground in front of him.

Then he stopped.

"Wait!" Mike said, pulling his hand away from Shannon. "We have no idea where they are . . . or do I?"

"What are you talking about?" asked Jeff. "You can't see through ice."

"No, but maybe I can sense them," Mike explained. He pressed a button on his Dino Jacket's zipper. **FWIP! FWIP! FWIP!** The stegosaurus-like plates burst out of the back of the high-tech hoodie again. "The heat spheres! When they were circling the argentinosaurus, my Dino Jacket could track their energy."

The plates on the back of his jacket began to glow with pale blue light, and Mike could feel sensors in his sleeves.

"There!" he pointed at Jeff's feet.

Jeff leaped backward just as one of the burrowing dinos burst through the ice, snapping its jaws. It was a narrow miss! Now that it was out in the open, Jeff could easily avoid it. He had plenty of practice with dinosaurs of all kinds.

Mike pointed at Shannon's feet. "One is coming up there!" he yelled.

Shannon was able to move out of the way easily. The dinosaurs continued to pop up and then burrow into the earth, again and again. Dino-Mike was able to predict their location each time with one hundred percent accuracy.

"Stay separated," said Jeff, "so that we can better fight off the attacks. As long as Mike can tell us where they're coming from, we should be okay."

Dino-Mike glanced over at the Bones siblings. They had stopped controlling the dinosaurs and were whispering to each other.

They're planning something, Mike thought. And just then, they stared back at him with evil smiles.

The brother and sister team thrust their fists toward the sky.

SMAAAAAAAAAASH!

All eight oryctodromeus burst from the ice, surrounding Dino-Mike! They snapped their jaws, showing off their glistening, razor-sharp teeth.

Is this how Dino-Mike goes extinct? Mike wondered.

Chapter 7

ICE TO THE RESCUE

SNAP! SNAP! SNAP! Dozens of deadly teeth snapped open and closed inches from Mike's face. He feared they would be the last thing he ever saw.

Mike shut his eyes and hoped for the best. But after a few moments, nothing had happened.

Dino-Mike slowly opened his eyes. The dozens of gnashing teeth were gone!

THWAP! THWAP! THWAP!

Mike turned his attention toward a nearby pelting sound. Jeff, Shannon, and Dr. Jiang were striking the dinos with barrage of snowballs. The startled dinosaurs quickly burrowed themselves back under the ice.

"WOO-HOO!" Jurassic Jeff shouted in victory.

The celebration didn't last. **CRACK! SMASH! BASH!** The dinosaurs quickly surfaced again, even angrier than before.

Dino-Mike noticed the orb-shaped heat spheres zipping closely behind each creature. Without hesitating, he scrambled to his feet and grabbed a chunk of ice.

Mike positioned himself in a batting stance his dad had showed him. When another dino popped out of the ground, Dino-Mike swung the long piece of ice just like he would a baseball bat.

SMAAAASH!

He smashed the heat sphere and watched its smoky trail travel to what Mike estimated should be about center field. Without its heat source, the dinosaur was hit with a cold blast of air and immediately went into survival mode. It quickly scurried back underground for warmth.

Mike knocked the other heat spheres out of the park as well. Soon all of the oryctodromeus were back underground.

Unable to control them, the Bones siblings blasted the dinosaurs back to the past. **POP! POP! POP!**

"Li Jing! Chiang!" Dr. Jiang shouted at his children. "Stop this foolishness."

"This is not foolishness, Father!" said his son. "What you did was foolish! We're just taking back what should have been ours!"

"Dinosaurs don't belong to anyone!" Shannon interrupted. "They were here long before we arrived, and they should never be in the hands of crazies like you two!"

"Dinos belong to anyone who can control them, little girl," said Chiang, "and that is us!"

"Well, it looks like you've failed to do that," said Jeff, pointing to where the oryctodromeus disappeared under the ice.

The Bones siblings started laughing.

"What's so funny?" asked Jeff. "You are out of those heat spheres. Any dinos you unearth will quickly freeze."

"There were other dinosaurs that were used to the most extreme and cold environments," replied Li Jing.

"Yes, plenty of dinosaurs inhabited cold environments," Shannon explained, "but not the extreme temperatures you find here in Antarctica."

"Wrong." The Boneses laughed.

While everyone was talking, Mike noticed Li Jing was busy looking at a small computer readout attached to her glove, like a high-tech watch or phone.

"They're crazy," said Jeff. "Nothing that ever roamed on land could withstand such extreme temperatures. If they don't have heat spheres to help them, they've got nothing."

Dino-Mike thought for a second. He remembered Atlantis and an encounter he had there with an underwater dinosaur.

"Um," Mike began, "maybe not on land, but what about —"

The Bones siblings thrust their hands into the air again, and the ice beneath everyone was beginning to crack.

CRRAAAAASH!

"Water!" Mike screamed.

Just then, the biggest underwater dinosaur he'd ever seen burst through the ice like a tidal wave!

Chapter 8

PLESIOSAUROMORPH

"Uh-oh!" said Shannon.

"Plesiosaurus!" yelled Jeff.

Mike watched the beast leap through the air. He could see its long, slender neck, body, and tail being propelled up by four large, flat, paddle-like arms.

"Actually, it's a plesiosauromorph!" Dino-Mike yelled back.

After his last encounter with an underwater dinosaur, Dino-Mike had done some research on them.

Mike knew the plesiosauromorph was an apex predator — a SUPER predator! The worst of the absolute worst. In other words, they were all in big, big trouble right about now.

Before anyone else could react, Dino-Mike pushed his group of friends back. The ice was cracking beneath their feet. Unfortunately, he didn't make it in time to get them to safety.

SMAAAAAASH!

The plesiosauromorph came crashing down, breaking up the ice all around them. Before they knew it, they were all on different slabs of ice.

They each held on for dear life as the slabs bobbed up and down like ice cubes in a glass.

Looking at the giant dinosaur — which must have measured fifty feet long — Dino-Mike could understand how some people believed sea monsters could exist. The proof was right in front of him!

"Shannon!" shouted Mike. "You need to get those gloves away from the Bones twins!"

Mike picked up Ahfu, who happened to be closest to him when the ice broke up, and threw him safely over to Shannon.

"How are we supposed to do that?" asked Shannon, catching the dog.

"The twins are busy controlling this monster!" Mike explained. "I'll distract them, but you guys need to get those gloves and take away their ability to control any more dinosaurs!"

"But Mike —" Shannon started.

"He's right, sis," Jeff interrupted. "This has to stop — now!"

Mike nodded back.

"Wait!" yelled out Shannon again in protest. "Be careful!"

Without answering, Dino-Mike jumped into action. He reached inside his jacket and pressed a button.

PFFFFFT!

The jacket tripled in size as it filled
with helium and lifted Dino-Mike off the
ice slab like a hot-air balloon.

Gaining the attention of the dinosaur by making himself the biggest target was exactly what Mike wanted. It didn't take long for the dinosaur to notice the giant green ball hovering in front of its eyes.

Dino-Mike had puffed up his jacket and figured he would outmaneuver and distract the dinosaur.

He couldn't have been more wrong.

He'd never seen a dinosaur move so fast! The long, slender flippers that were the size of boats smacked the ice and water as it came toward Mike.

CHOMP!! The plesiosauromorph chomped down on Dino-Mike.

Mike wasn't worried . . . yet. His high-tech Dino Jacket had once withstood a bite from an angry triceratops.

Suddenly, the plesiosauromorph leaped into the air, and then arched its long body and dove back toward the water below.

Uh-oh! thought Mike. This is not what he had planned. He was about to be taken to the plesiosauromorph's own turf deep below the sea.

Now Mike was worried.

Chapter 9
DINO-SUB

Wait! Mike suddenly thought. A plan popped into his head like a light switch flicking on.

After Dino-Mike's most recent adventure, Dr. Broome had upgraded the Dino Jacket with several new technologies, including SCUBA mode!

"Not that you would ever need it," Mike remembered Dr. Broome saying. "But you never know."

You never know, Dino-Mike thought.

The surface of the icy ocean water rushed toward him. Mike reached into his jacket and tried to remember where the button was. *There!*

BEEEEEP! Mike hit the button just as he hit the water.

FWOOOOSH! All of the air suddenly rushed out of his jacket. As it did, Mike could feel the jacket changing shape.

As the plesiosauromorph dived deeper and deeper, Dino-Mike held his breath. But just as he couldn't hold his breath any longer, he realized that he didn't have to. His Dino Jacket had become a deep-ocean diving suit. He was safe, but for how long?

He was still trapped in the jaws of a

behemoth dinosaur, after all.

Then, **WHUMP!!**

Suddenly, everything went dark as the jaws of the plesiosauromorph snapped shut around him. Everything was still and quiet.

Where am I? Mike wondered. Then he realized. "Ewwwww . . ."

Dino-Mike was inside the dinosaur's mouth. But he didn't have time to stop and think about how gross that actually was. Mike could see that he was about to be swallowed!

To add even more disturbing news, Mike could see the inside of the dino was starting to spark! Little arcs of electricity and a sound like water being sucked down a drain — no, a vacuum!

The Bones siblings were about to teleport this dinosaur! Mike was in big trouble! He was about to be swallowed and teleported! He didn't know which was more frightening!

Just then, Dino-Mike felt his feet being sucked into the dino's throat. Then his legs. Then his waist. Then —

He was stuck!

Dino-Mike could feel the underwater dinosaur begin to buck and jerk. He felt the dinosaur's throat begin to cough and spit. The plesiosauromorph was choking! Mike didn't want harm the dinosaur, but he instantly thought, *Ha! I've got you now!*

Mike figured at this point, since the dinosaur could not eat him, it would have to expel him. He didn't have to wait long. He looked out the view window and could see the plesiosauromorph had opened its mouth and water was rushing in. Mike braced himself, as he was sure things were about to get violent.

What happened next could only be described as sneezing underwater, but it was a very large dinosaur so the sneeze was very powerful.

FWOOOSH! Mike was pushed out with the force and velocity of a bullet as he soared out of the dinosaur's mouth and back into open water.

As the Dino Jacket tumbled end over
end through the water, Dino-Mike was
being thrown around inside his own
jacket. Good thing it was all soft and
padded in there!

Mike soared through the water, splashing around in the ocean.

As he did, Mike heard a loud **POP!** He was sure the dinosaur was gone — transported out of there by the Bones siblings.

After a few more tumbles, Mike thought he was going to get seasick but did his best to control the jacket. He needed to get back and help his friends take down the Bones siblings.

There was just one problem: he had been thrown and tossed around so much, he couldn't tell where the surface was located. If he went the wrong way, he might not be able to find the surface.

Mike looked in every direction, but couldn't tell which way was up.

His air supply was running out fast!

Chapter 10

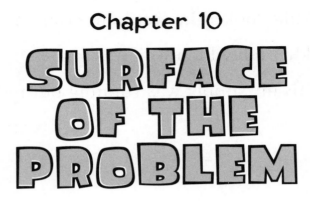

SURFACE OF THE PROBLEM

Dino-Mike needed to find a way to the surface. He wasn't worried about breaking through the ice — his Dino Jacket could handle that task. But he needed to solve this problem first.

Mike squinted and peered in every direction for a clue. *What is that?* he wondered, spotting a blackish blur in the distance.

FSSSSSSHT!

He let out a bit of air from the jacket to propel him in the direction of the object. As he got closer, the blur became many blurs, and they were all swimming in one direction — up!

As he got even closer he could tell that they were penguins! The penguins were playing and fishing and frolicking in the ocean. They were everywhere.

They must sense the dinosaur is gone, Mike thought, watching the animals play in the water.

Mike quickly followed the direction of the penguins and surfaced! He could see the sky!

BEEP! Dino-Mike pressed another button on his sleeve. The Dino Jacket transformed from SCUBA Mode back to normal.

He was thankful for the waddling little creatures because they just saved his life. Sensing no threat from him, the penguins continued to frolic and play and dive and shoot up out of the water all around him. It was an incredible sight, one he preferred much more than being chased by a plesiosauromorph or T. rex.

The thought jolted him back to reality. He needed to get back to his friends!

He arrived just in time to witness the best thing he could imagine. Li Jing and her brother were arguing. They were calling each other names and blaming each other for all the things they thought the other did wrong.

Jeff and Shannon had Li Jing unmasked and ungloved!

Jeff was holding her hands behind her back as Shannon was taking off Li Jing's glove. She was now powerless and unable to control any more dinosaurs. Li Jing's father was right behind them, and Mike could tell he was scolding his daughter for her bad actions against all of them.

Mike looked around for the big baddie himself, the mastermind behind all of this, Chiang Bones. He was on the ground, struggling with Ahfu. The dog had managed to take him down and was standing on Chiang's chest, barking at him.

"Get off me, you stupid dog!" he yelled at him.

"This is why he never liked you! This is all your fault! I never should have listened to you!" yelled Li Jing at her brother.

Mike remembered that Jeff had said all they had to do was get the siblings to argue, and it was working!

This was Mike's chance! He rushed at Chiang, trying to get the brother's gloves before he could do any more damage.

"You almost had me Dino-Mike!" Chiang yelled as Mike closed in. "But there will be another time!"

A split second later, **FWOOOOOSH!**

A hurricane-force wind ripped across the landscape again.

Then a swirling, sideways tornado of air opened into an interdimensional portal, sucking Chiang Bones inside.

Mike raced over to Li Jing and pointed a finger at her. "Tell me where your brother is right now!" he demanded.

"Never!" she replied. "What we are doing is important. My brother and I may not get along all the time, but I will not tell you where he is."

"You shame me, daughter," muttered Dr. Jiang.

"Just great," said Mike, throwing his hands up in the air. "Now we have to wait for Chiang to strike again.

"Maybe not. Has anyone noticed that he leaves a clue every time he or one of the dinosaurs disappears?" said Shannon, pointing to some grayish white powder on the ice. "Too bad we don't know where this dust is from — it might give us a clue as to where they have their hideout."

Jurassic Jeff kneeled next to the powder. "It's not like any soil I've seen on Earth," he said.

Dr. Jiang rubbed a bit between his fingers. "That's because this soil cannot be found here."

Mike agreed. "Antarctica's soil is covered in lots of ice and snow."

"This soil is not from Antarctica,"
said Dr. Jiang

"Father, no!" pleaded Li Jing.

Despite his daughter's protest, Dr.
Jiang continued, "I'm sorry, daughter.
What you and your brother have done
must stop."

He turned to Mike and sifted the powder into Mike's gloved hand.

"Where is it from, Doctor? Australia? South America?" asked Mike.

"No," answered Dr. Jiang. "This is not soil from Earth."

"What?" said Mike, confused. "What are you talking about?"

"This soil is from the Moon," explained Dr. Jiang.

Dino-Mike turned to the group. "We better start digging out my dad," he said. "I'm think I'm going to need his permission to go where we're headed."

GLOSSARY

Antarctica (ant-ARK-tih-kah)—continent at the South Pole

fossil (FAWSS-uhl)—the remains, impression, or trace of a living thing of a former geologic age, like a dinosaur bone

helium (HEE-lee-uhm)—a lightweight, colorless gas that does not burn

horizon (huh-RYE-zuhn)—the line where the sky and the earth or sea seem to meet

Jurassic Period (juh-RASS-ik PEER-ee-uhd)—a period of time about 200 to 144 million years ago

paleontologist (pay-lee-uhn-TOL-uh-jist)—a scientist who deals with fossils and other life-forms

velocity (vuh-LOSS-uh-tee)—a measurement of both the speed and direction an object is moving

DINO JOKES!

Q: What do you call a dinosaur that steps on a car?
A: Tyrannosaurus Wrecks.

Q: What toys do dinosaurs play with?
A: Tricera-tops.

Q: What do you call a dinosaur stuck in a glacier?
A: A fossicle.

Q: Who is the fastest dinosaur?
A: A prontosaurus.

Q: What days of the week do raptors eat their food?
A: Chewsday.

Q: Where was the T. rex when the sun set?

A: In the dark.

Q: Why do museums display old dinosaur bones?

A: They can't afford the new ones.

Q: Where does a triceratops sit?

A: On its tricera-bottom.

Q: What makes more noise than a dinosaur?

A: Ten dinosaurs!

Q: What do you call a dinosaur that talks and talks and talks?

A: A dino-bore.

ABOUT THE AUTHOR

Bronx, New York–born writer and artist Franco Aureliani has been drawing comics since he could hold a crayon. Currently residing in upstate New York with his wife, Ivette, and son, Nicolas, he spends most of his days in his Batcave-like studio where he works on comics projects. In 1995, Franco founded Blindwolf Studios, an independent art studio where he and fellow creators can create children's comics. Franco is the creator, artist, and writer of Weirdsville, L'il Creeps, and Eagle All Star, as w   nd writer of Patrick

Franco recently
Superman Family A
Titans by DC Com   lboy
and Aw Yeah Com   ics.
When he's not wr   nco
teaches high-scho